D0351858

To
Princess Dress
Pasta Palace

For David

Scholastic Children's Books,
Commonwealth House, 1-19 New Oxford Street,
London WC1A 1NU, UK
a division of Scholastic Ltd

London – New York – Toronto – Sydney – Auckland
Mexico City – New Delhi – Hong Kong

First published in hardback by Scholastic Ltd, 1999
This paperback edition published by Scholastic Ltd, 2002

ISBN 0 439 99874 3

Printed and bound in China

2 4 6 8 10 9 7 5 3 1

Princess Dress

Sue Heap

The sun rose up on Pasta Palace.

Inside Pasta Palace,
Princess Dress woke up.
She was very excited
because today was
her birthday.

incess Dress princess Dress princess Dress princess Dress Princess Dress pr

Princess Dress

She
wondered
which dress to
wear to her party.

She called for her seven servants and
seven best dresses.

She liked her red dress
but it was too itchy and hot!

She loved the orange dress
she'd worn last year, but now
it was just too small!

She wasn't sure about her yellow dress
because it was too fussy!

She didn't like
her green dress,
it was too plain!

Her blue dress was fine
but, oh dear, it had
a big tear!

She looked in the mirror at her indigo dress. It might fit her next year but now it was much too big!

She really hated the violet dress. It was too grown up and not much fun on her birthday.

Happy Birthday

To our dear
Princess Dress
Happy Birthday
x love from
us all x

So she went to the party just as she was, in her pyjamas! Princess Dress opened her birthday present. What could it be . . . ?

. . . a brand new party dress.

The moon rose up on Pasta Palace
and the party was still going on.

Her new dress shimmered and
sparkled as she danced.

And Princess Dress
was very very happy.